What Happens in Winter?

Birds in Winter

by Jenny Fretland VanVoorst

Bullfrog
Books

Ideas for Parents and Teachers

Bullfrog Books let children practice reading informational text at the earliest reading levels. Repetition, familiar words, and photo labels support early readers.

Before Reading

• Discuss the cover photo. What does it tell them?

• Look at the picture glossary together. Read and discuss the words.

Read the Book

• "Walk" through the book and look at the photos. Let the child ask questions. Point out the photo labels.

• Read the book to the child, or have him or her read independently.

After Reading

• Prompt the child to think more. Ask: What kinds of birds have you seen in winter near your house?

Bullfrog Books are published by Jump!
5357 Penn Avenue South
Minneapolis, MN 55419
www.jumplibrary.com

Library of Congress Cataloging-in-Publication Data

Names: Fretland VanVoorst, Jenny, 1972– author.
Title: Birds in winter / by Jenny Fretland VanVoorst.
Description: Minneapolis, MN: Jump!, Inc. [2017]
Series: Bullfrog books. What happens in winter?
"Bullfrog Books are published by Jump!."
Audience: Ages 5–8. | Audience: K to grade 3.
Includes bibliographical references and index.
Identifiers: LCCN 2016002932
ISBN 9781620313947 (hardcover: alk. paper)
ISBN 9781620314982 (paperback)
ISBN 9781624964411 (ebook)
Subjects: LCSH:
Birds—Behavior—Juvenile literature.
Birds—Migration—Juvenile literature.
Winter—Juvenile literature.
Classification:
LCC QL698.3.F684 2017 | DDC 598.156—dc23
LC record available at http://lccn.loc.gov/2016002932

Series Designer: Ellen Huber
Book Designer: Leah Sanders
Photo Researcher: Kirsten Chang

Photo Credits: All photos by Shutterstock except: Alamy, 5, 16, 23br; Getty Images, 14–15, 20–21, 23tr, 23tl; Thinkstock, 8–9, 10–11, 12, 23bl.

Printed in the United States of America at Corporate Graphics in North Mankato, Minnesota.

Table of Contents

Stay or Go?

Winter is coming.

The birds must leave.

It is too cold.

Food is scarce.

Geese fly south.
They make a V.

The goose at
the point works
the hardest.

She is tired.

Soon another
goose will take
her place.

9

Some birds
stick around.

11

Sparrows flock together for warmth.

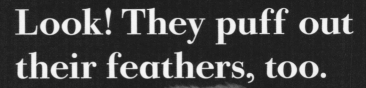
Look! They puff out their feathers, too.

13

Birds must eat
more to stay warm.

Cardinals eat
winter berries.

They eat birdseed.

Tom feeds the birds.
He gives them suet.

suet

He gives them seeds.

seeds

Soon the weather
will warm.

Birds will return
from the South.

Look for the robin.

It's a sign that spring is here!

Birds of Winter

goldfinch

bluebird

cardinal

oriole

Picture Glossary

cardinal
A North American bird often seen in the winter; the male is bright red.

robin
A large bird with a grayish back and head and a brick red breast.

flock
To gather or move in a crowd.

suet
A hard block of animal fat that is often fed to birds for extra energy in the winter.

Index

To Learn More

Learning more is as easy as 1, 2, 3.

1) Go to www.factsurfer.com

2) Enter "birdsinwinter" into the search box.

3) Click the "Surf" button to see a list of websites.

With factsurfer.com, finding more information is just a click away.